教孩子說一口流利英語

從建立自信、認讀拼音到場景練習

English Speaker

陳美心 著

U0061080

萬里機構

自序

　　本書的訓練課程以培訓英語聽、説、讀及寫能力為學習骨幹；前作《快快樂樂學英語拼音》*Happy English Phonetic Learners* 讓學生及讀者鞏固了聆聽英語的基礎，此書則是強化説話能力。

　　「講」是活生生的，有生命氣息的及有交流的。適時的表達亦是與他人建立融洽及長久關係中不可或缺的橋樑。我們可以通過講話來分享自身的夢想、經驗和娛樂。

書內每個課堂，分別指導孩子掌握講話的節奏、詞彙的重音、語調及語氣表達的技巧。小朋友若能持之以恆地鍛煉，相信交友能力方面必有所提升，從而擴展交友圈。現在，讓我  們一起在學習中理解彼此的感受，只有真誠及有智慧的對話，生活才有價值。

目錄
CONTENTS

CHAPTER

 個人準備篇

CHAPTER

 說話技巧篇

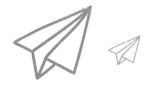

CHAPTER

3 場景練習篇

CHAPTER

4 演說練習及比賽篇

CHAPTER

個人準備篇

說得一口流利的英語，

除了英語技巧運用得宜外，

個人的準備也很重要，

父母嘗試協助了解子女的情緒及感覺，

保持好奇心，

讓他們建立說英語的自信心，

是增強英語聽、說、讀、寫的第一步。

LESSON 1

SUBJECT: _____

DATE: _____

OBJECTIVES:

認識自己的感覺及情緒，明白
學英語的重要性，提升自信！

NOTES

　　建議讓小朋友熟知自己的感覺，了解自己的
情緒，利用最原始的自身感覺，運用於英語的
聽、說、讀、寫等方面。

　　小朋友學習英語表達時，要注意以下數點，
梳理自己的感覺及情緒，以提升英語學習。

❶ 察覺情緒 ——由於父母的壓力或家庭給予的期
　望，小朋友容易壓抑自己的情緒，不易表達出
　來。可引導小朋友懂得察覺平日的感受，了解
　內心所想，找出自己的優點。

❷ **辨別情緒** —— 察覺情緒後，協助小朋友辨別及梳理自身的各種情緒，加強學習英語的決心。

❸ **接納情緒** —— 妥善接納自己的情緒，放開胸襟，表達自己，向着自己的目標邁進。

❹ **用故事或誦材表達感受** —— 在演講或唸英文詩歌時，適當地加入自己的感受、情緒及語調，賦予作品個人化的表達。

利用詞彙庫豐富小朋友感覺及情緒的用詞，加深認識情緒，從而更能表達出來。

emotion	情緒	kind	善良
happy	快樂	sensitive	敏感
sad	憂愁	considerate	考量
angry	憤怒	cool	冷漠
shy	害羞	brilliant	出色／有才氣
mild	溫和	excellent	優異
fantastic	幻想		

TIPS

❶ 了解子女的特質及喜好 ——父母要了解子女的獨特才能，例如運動或語言方面，給予適當的栽培及培養，以免人云亦云報讀過多興趣班。

❷ 多觀察，傾談心中所想 ——溝通是雙向的，多細聽子女的想法，喜歡參加英語班？還是田徑班？若子女年紀尚幼，可透過繪畫來表達自己。

❸ 多說故事啟發創意 ——以圖書為溝通媒介，挑選子女合適的英文圖書，朗讀一段後，針對內容設定問題，啟發子女的想像空間及創意。

　　建議家長以身作則，在日常生活中指導小朋友，幫助他們建立說話的良好習慣，例如學習問候他人、與人打招呼，注意自己及別人的感受，培養互動溝通，擴闊社交圈子，養成不害羞的性格。

　　如小朋友未能察覺或辨別自己的情緒，家長可以鼓勵的說話回應，例如：

- 雖然我們未完全了解你的想法，但謝謝你與我分享，我們可以再一起談談。

- 當你想分享的時候,我們可以再交談。

　　以上的回應,令小朋友慢慢放開心窗,無憂無慮地傾談,話匣子打開了,英語說話可以由此訓練下去。

TRAINING

對話練習

"Where do you live?"
"What is your job?"
"How is your family?"

　　跟別人交談是一件很開心的事。以上每句說話正是拉近彼此距離的軟工具,能建構大家的親和感。英語會話是學習說話的最佳範本,不單可在人際關係裏活學活用,亦是療癒個人心靈上的潤滑劑。

以下是 Miss Chan 於香港會議展覽中心，與一位家長就「如何增強説英語自信心」而展開的對話。

Miss Chan held an English Training presentation at the Hong Kong Exhibition and Convention Centre.

Listen to the dialogue.

Miss Chan (MC)

Adult Speaker: Audrea (A)

A: Hi, Miss Chan. Nice to meet you here. I have been reading your book since your centre's opening ceremony in 2000. Thank you for delivering this valuable talk about Little English Speakers Training for Hong Kong parents and kids. Are there any ways to boost children's confidence in speaking English?

MC: Thank you for your support. Actually, self-confidence means to trust in your judgement, capacities and abilities. Building self-confidence is like cutting and polishing a diamond. A jeweller must cut the right number of facets and then polish the diamond until it shines brightly. With a positive attitude we can master our skills and achieve our goals. If children try their best and concentrate on their lessons, they will certainly succeed in speaking.

A: Is it difficult to build children's self-confidence? Our days can be so chaotic and messy as we deal with our children's issues both at school and at home.

MC: That's a good question. As a mother and a teacher, making time for educating children can be difficult. But with love, we can certainly in boosting children's confidence. To achieve this, children could develop some good habits, like these:

1. Regular exercise such as swimming and running, build strong lungs, vital for breath control and voice projection, both important for clear and confident speech. Children need energy to study and practice.

2. A balanced healthy diet rich in fruit, vegetables, proteins and good carbohydrates is the way to keep children active throughout the day.

3. Positive experiences that build a child's sense of self-worth make them resilient when faced with challenges or set-backs. Winning a competition is a good example of this.

4. Success depends on a good support network, from our families, classmates and close friends.

A: That's great. Thank you, Miss Chan, for your kindness to our children. I look forward to the next time you share your insights with us.

MC: See you all next time.

EXERCISE

理解及練習

A. 閱讀理解

Based on the dialogue, briefly answer questions 1-3, then select the correct answers for the multiple choice questions 4-5.

1. What is self-confidence?

2. Why are healthy diets important?

3. Name two exercises that you can do every day.

4. According to Miss Chan, which one of the following is bright and shiny?
   a. a star   b. the moon
   c. a ring   d. a diamond

5. Which of the following does Miss Chan say is the best thing to help children learn?
   a. a toy   b. a pet   c. love   d. candy

B. 朗讀生字

Words	IPA	中文解釋
reader	/ˈriː.dər/	讀者
confidence	/ˈkɒn.fɪ.dəns/	信心
increase	/ɪnˈkriːs/	加強
talk	/tɔːk/	演講
master	/ˈmɑː.stər/	掌握
skill	/skɪl/	技術
clearly	/ˈklɪə.li/	清楚地
stage	/steɪdʒ/	舞台
positive	/ˈpɒz.ə.tɪv/	正面

C. 日常練習

1. Read the dialogue once and record it.

2. Use the words above to create a story for your individual presentation.

美心老師格言

每天需要創意（Innovation）及創造力（Creativity），為生活創造生命力。

SUBJECT:

DATE:

OBJECTIVES:

由認識身體開始，表達自己，建立說英語的自信！

　　小朋友是很單純的個體，由呱呱落地開始，身體與他們相連，是他們最熟悉的，藉着身體作為媒介來表達自己，掌握以英語表達的能力，可提升聯想力及自信心。

NOTES

學習要點

❶ **多認識及運用身體各部分，表達自己** —— 身體是重要的一部分，小朋友若充分了解身體，能靈活運用各身體部分表達心中所想。

❷ **讓小朋友感受英語是生活的一部分** —— 身體作為一個媒介、一項工具，與小朋友的生活連成一線，讓他們在日常中習慣地活用英語，獲得其他人的認同，建立自信。

利用詞彙庫豐富小朋友有關身體的用詞，提升英語表達力。

face	臉	lip	嘴唇
wrist	腕	hair	頭髮
chin	下巴	hand	手
eye	眼睛	chest	胸
finger	手指		

TIPS

家長錦囊

　　讓小朋友透過跑步、遊戲、大笑及唱歌，與子女一起同呼同吸、同唱同笑，藉着身體互動溝通，互相感受及磨合，認識身體的協調性（coordination）和運動技能（motor skills），趟開心扉，營造輕鬆的氛圍，建立雙方良好的溝通，傾談自然暢順得多。

　　透過身體的動能（kinesthetic in nature），對小朋友學習英語有以下好處：

❶ 通過學習觸摸及感觀意識（senses），令學習英語更有成效 ——父母與子女透過身體的觸感，建立一份親密的感覺，這種感覺意識的聯繫，營造一個輕鬆學習英語的環境，擺脫硬綁綁的傳統學習模式。

❷ 小朋友完成身體學習體驗後，更容易理解教學的題目或目標 ——當小朋友的內心無約束，能夠自由奔放地盡情玩樂，以輕鬆的心情取代學習新事物的不安感，令他們更容易領會學習的方向及目標。

❸ **建立身體和英文生字的聯繫性，有助發展日後
聽、說、讀及寫的能力** —— 可以用感覺或身體
部位來牢記英文生字，活學活用，增加創意及
聯想力之餘，也富有趣味性，例如：

- head 與 floor（我的頭碰到地板，很痛呢！）
- eye 與 cup（杯內的水濺到我的眼睛了！）
- nose 與 book（厚厚的書本撞到我的鼻子。）
- mouth 與 tissue（進食後要用紙巾抹嘴呀！）
- neck 與 pen（頸項上掛了一枝有趣的筆。）

父母也可透過生動的故事，與子女認識以下
身體的詞語，豐富詞彙。

ear	耳朵	stomach	胃
thumb	拇指	nose	鼻
arm	臂	nail	指甲
mouth	口	forearm	前臂
leg	腿		

TRAINING

對話練習

面對他人説英説是需要勇氣，多鼓勵孩子運用英語與別人交談，能贏得個人的自信心。

A Class with Miss Chan

Miss Chan (MC)

Little English Speakers: Heather (H), Lucas (L) and Macy (M)

M: Hi, everyone. We are going to have a farm visit in Lam Tei in two weeks. Ted, who is not from Hong Kong and is a native English speaker, will join our activity. Any suggestions for the visit?

H: (Raises her hand) Oh, that sounds great! We will get to speak English more often. May I see the site map? It must be challenging.

M: It's my turn. There's a Chinese temple below the farm near the Light Transit Railway. I think we should bring our umbrellas. You know, it's been raining every day this month.

L: Can we have breakfast before going to the farm? I am always hungry! (All burst into laughter.)

MC: So, who will be the project leader this time?

H: (Stands up) Miss Chan, I think I can do it. But I'm a bit nervous and hesitant when speaking English with foreigners.

L: Heather, take it easy. Let's practice more after lunch together!

MC: Good Job. Let's get cracking!

個人準備篇

EXERCISE

理解及練習

A. 閱讀理解

1. What is the meaning of the expression "Let's get cracking" ?

2. What type of building is situated below the farm?
   a. a shop   b. a salon
   c. a Chinese temple   d. a canteen

3. Who becomes the project leader of the farm visit?
   a. Heather   b. Lucas
   c. Miss Chan   d. Macy

4. Who will help Heather practice English for the farm visit?
   a. Macy   b. Miss Chan
   c. Melody   d. Lucas

5. If you were the project leader, what skills would you have to acquire? (Refer to Lesson One)

B. 朗讀生字

Words	IPA	中文解釋
farm visit	/fɑːm/ /ˈvɪz.ɪt/	農莊探訪
foreigner	/ˈfɒr.ə.nər/	外國人
Chinese temple	/tʃaɪˈniːz/ /ˈtem.pəl/	廟宇
Light Transit Railway	/laɪt/ /ˈtræn.zɪt/ /ˈreɪl.weɪ/	輕鐵
project	/ˈprɒdʒ.ekt/	項目
leader	/ˈliː.dər/	負責人
practice	/ˈpræk.tɪs/	練習
hesitation	/ˌhez.ɪˈteɪ.ʃən/	猶疑
ability	/əˈbɪl.ə.ti/	能力

C. 日常練習

1. Read the dialogue once and record it.

2. Use the above words to create a story for your individual presentation.

美心老師格言

每天 2P（Patient 忍耐 + Perseverance 堅持）是 成功的要素。

NOTES

LESSON 3

SUBJECT:

DATE:

OBJECTIVES:

好奇心是説話的原動力！

　　每個小朋友都是活潑好動，有着自己喜愛的興趣活動、玩具或寵物，充滿強烈的求知慾。曾經有一名學生上課時帶着一隻玩具蜥蝪，原來他很喜歡爬蟲類，我就以他的喜好，由蜥蝪開始説起英語來。漸漸，他愛上説英語。

　　父母可發掘子女有興趣的話題或嗜好，透過朗讀英語圖書或對話等創造説英語的機會，説不定他們會説的比你想像的還多呢！

NOTES

學習要點

刺激學習的動機——對大部分人來説，針對自己有興趣的事物來學習，是一種很大的推動力，尤其小朋友的耐性有限，以他們喜歡的玩具、喜好及寵物談起，加上圖書的視覺刺激，可增強小朋友學習英語的聽、講、寫能力。

TIPS

❶ 發掘小朋友的興趣——從日常生活上多觀察子女的喜好、興趣等，了解他們內心的所想及感覺，小朋友感受到父母的關心，自然願意隨父母一起探索。

❷ 引發小朋友的好奇心——帶領子女到不同的地方或場景，引發他們的好奇心，大人與小孩一起去摸索、去發問、去滿足彼此的好奇心，在父母帶領之下，開啟小朋友說英語的契機。

❸ 多給予正面鼓勵——父母正面的回應、鼓勵及讚賞，能增進親子感情；而多閱讀有興趣的書籍，也能加強好奇心及子女日後的自學能力。

　　舉個例子，農莊是小朋友喜愛的地方，父母可藉着到農莊遊玩，一同觸摸檸檬葉（用手搓揉會有檸檬香味），透過觸感及嗅覺的刺激，能增強小朋友的思維及說話動機，自我的感覺豐富了，才能懂得如何用英語表達出來。

　　回到家裏，可引導子女繪畫農莊的所見所聞，透過畫作的聯想，父母可讓子女用英語說出自己的感受、事物或經過，豐富他們的英語詞彙，甚至讓創意鞏固英語演說及寫作，從小栽培，成就他們未來的英語創作。

TRAINING

A Conversation About the 3Cs

Miss Chan (MC)

Christy (C) - She is the mother of Little English Speakers

Beavis and Charlotte

C: Miss Chan, thank you for teaching my children English Speaking. Beavis was selected as a Primary 2 school representative in the Annual Hong Kong Schools Music and Speech Festival 2021. My husband and I are a working couple; can you give me some tips for educating my children at home?

MC: Many thanks indeed. Throughout my years teaching kids, I've learned that the 3Cs are vital for a happy and healthy life.

C: Miss Chan, what are the 3Cs? Will this be difficult for us as we are not well-educated?

MC: The "3Cs" mean cultivating Curiosity, Compassion and Constructive mindsets in children. These three qualities are critical not just to develop healthy childhood growth, but also for their adult lives. Curiousity makes children eager to know more. For example, our visit to the organic farm made children want to learn even more about the plants and insects at the farm. That, in turn, will lead them into an interest in science. I know your elder son Alfie likes lizards and has one as a pet. Learning more about how to care for his pet will motivate him to learn more about these fascinating reptiles.

C: Yes, I agree with your point. After joining in your activity, Alfie became more talkative and was thrilled to share his experiences at the organic farm. He goes to the library and borrows books related to insects and even makes models of things he's interested in. He makes good use of the 10 words that Miss Chan teaches, writing them in his notebook and revisiting them often. It's been really effective in increasing his English proficiency, especially as it doesn't force him, but rather guides him naturally, thanks to you.

MC: With the right encouragement, kids' creativity can be unlimited. Let's share more about this next time.

All: Thank you, Miss Chan.

EXERCISE

理解及練習

A. 閱讀理解

1. Who is in the Annual Hong Kong Schools Music and Speech Festival 2021?

2. Name the 3Cs. According to Miss Chan, why is curiosity important for children's growth?

3. Describe Alfie's English learning efforts.

4. Share your experiences in learning English. Do you think your English is good? Why?

5. Write a story about your favorite pet or toy in 100 words. Be sure to describe it!.

B. 朗讀生字

Words	IPA	中文解釋
motive	/ˈməʊ.tɪv/	原動力
curiosity	/ˌkjʊə.riˈɒs.ə.ti/	好奇心
compassion	/kəmˈpæʃ.ən/	有同情心
constructive	/kənˈstrʌk.tɪv/	對人有助益
plant	/plɑːnt/	植物
insect	/ˈɪn.sekt/	昆蟲
organic farm	/ɔːˈgæn.ɪk/ /fɑːm/	有機農場
incentive	/ɪnˈsen.tɪv/	誘因
thirst for knowledge	/θɜːst/ /əv/ /ˈnɒl.ɪdʒ/	求知慾

C. 日常練習

1. Read the above dialogue and record it.

2. Use the words above to create a story for your individual presentation.

NOTES

. . . .

個人準備篇

CHAPTER

說話技巧篇

掌握基本的英語說話技巧、

學好國際音標（I.P.A.），

能夠把英文字讀得準、讀得好。

讓學生掌握及運用正確的英語，

提出幾點說英語的小貼士，

日常多加訓練，配合熟讀英語拼音，

能夠吐字清晰，發音準確。

SUBJECT:

DATE:

OBJECTIVES:

掌握基本英語說話技巧

學習英語說話有以下的心法：

1. 融入英國的文化，找尋英語的旋律及掌握節拍及重音變化的方式。

2. 恆常鍛煉英語國際音標。

3. 清楚分辨英語聽、説、讀、寫的本質：聆聽及閱讀是「輸入」（input），説話及寫作是「輸出」（output）。

4. 培養樂觀及關懷他人的愉悦心，真心真意地和他人溝通。

NOTES

❶ 專注地聆聽對方的話語，包括如何說及怎樣回答。

❷ 持之以恆的練習方法：

  i. 要習慣聆聽及朗讀不同場境的會話。

  ii. 讓孩子到劇場或閱讀劇本的人物對話，了解他人（角色）為甚麼用這樣方式表達或演繹。

  iii. 多參與戲劇團體舉辦的戲劇課程或語言藝術工作坊，學習如何認識自己及擴闊思維。

  iv. 多與小朋友進行睡前對話，加深父母與子女間的連繫。

TIPS

❶ 在家裏，家長可朗讀故事書的章節，然後讓小朋友跟着朗讀。

❷ 平日可帶小朋友參與音樂及戲劇活動，練習聆聽旋律及劇場角色的對話，學習專注。

TRAINING

　　可在課餘時間，與同學一起創作會話故事及多作演練，例如慶祝生日。

　　生日人人都有，但感受各有不同，可以寫出自己的故事，藉此訓練說話技巧能力。我們可想一想自己對生日有何感覺，然後寫出對話。

Characters: Mum(M), Daughter(D), Papa (Dad)

The Time: At night

Place: Home

Mood: Sweet, warm and full of love

Title: My Birthday Cake

Mum and her daughter have come home from school.

D: I've been so tired all day. What a crazy school test schedule! (She dumps her school bags and belongings on the floor and goes to sleep on the sofa without changing her clothes.)

(Mum and Papa are preparing something special in the kitchen. They walk to the sofa.)

Dad: Wake up, please. (He says this gently.)

D: (She opens her eyes and lets out a sound of surprise.)
Wow, wow, wow! Look! My dream cake! It's made of rainbow colours red, orange, yellow, green, blue, purple - like my fairy dress, and it's full of coloured fruit candies - apple, banana, peppermint and grape flavours. On the top of the cake, there is a chocolate label writing "Happy Birthday, Sweet Girl"! I love it, Papa and Mum!. (D kisses and hugs Mum and Papa.)

M: I love your big eyes and sweet smile since I first saw you. Thank you for being our darling daughter. Throughout all these years, from the day you were born till now, you've always made us proud. (Mum's eyes are filled with tears.)

D: Thanks Papa and Mum for your caring. I love the two of you with all my heart. (D makes a wish and blows out the candles.) You will always be my birthday presents!

All: Let's have a wonderful and healthy life together, forever!

NOTES

LESSON 5

SUBJECT: DATE:

OBJECTIVES:

掌握發音 IPA

　　學習語言的心法，最重要是學懂感受他人説話時的情感，以及在對話時的發音、單字及文法，這些都是增強英語表達力的竅訣。

NOTES
學 習 要 點

A. 有效地掌握讀 IPA 的竅門：

❶ 先將 a‑z 的字母先寫一遍

a b c d e f g h i j k l m
n o p q r s t u v w x y z （26 個）

❷ 用紅筆圈出 a e i o u 的字母（母音）

ⓐ b c d ⓔ f g h ⓘ j k l m
n ⓞ p q r s t ⓤ v w x y z （5 個）

❸ 用黑筆或藍筆圈出 b c d f g h j k l m n p q r s t v w x y z 餘下的字母（子音），如下圖：

a b c d e f g h i j k l m n o p q r s t u v w x y z （21個）

❹ 熟讀子母音（可參考陳美心編著：《快快樂樂樂英語拼音》，萬里機構，第 12- 17 頁）

❺ 音節遊戲 —— 將已學習的子音及母音用遊戲方式和同學們一起練習，以下是其中一種合併方法及讀法，多朗讀、多演練，有助加強記憶之餘，在生活上亦可活學活用。

教孩子說 一口流利英語

LMNOP

說話技巧篇

子音	母音	字母	IPA	生字	解釋	創作句子	IPA
b	ei a	**ay**	bei	**bay**	海灣	**I love a clean bay.**	aɪ lʌv ə kliːn beɪ.
c	ei a	**ay**	cei	/	/	/	/
d	ei a	**ay**	dei	**day**	日子	**My day is full of joy.**	maɪ deɪ ɪz fʊl ɒv dʒɔɪ.
f	ei a	**ay**	fei	/	/	/	/
g	ei a	**ay**	gei	**gay**	開心	**What a gay time I had!**	wɒt ə geɪ taɪm aɪ hæd?
h	iː e	**e**	hiː	**he**	他	**He is a good guy.**	hiː ɪz ə gʊd gaɪ.
j	iː e	**ea**	jiːn	**jean**	牛仔褲	**His jeans are fashionable.**	hɪz dʒiːnz ɑː ˈfæʃnəbl.

子音	母音	字母	IPA	生字	解釋	創作句子	IPA
k	iː e	ee	kiːn	keen	渴望	She is keen to learn.	ʃiː ɪz kiːn tuː lɜːn.
l	iː e	ea	liːn	lean	依靠	A cat leans on the sofa.	ə kæt liːnz ɒn ðə ˈsəʊfə.
m	iː e	ee	miːt	meet	見面	Tom and Mary meet in the MTR station.	Tɒm ænd ˈMeəri miːt ɪn ðə ɛm-tiː-ɑː ˈsteɪʃən.
n	ai i	i	nain	nine	九	We have nine toys in our playroom.	wiː hæv naɪn tɔɪz ɪn ˈaʊə ˈpleɪrʊm.
p	ai i	i	pain	pine	松樹	Pines can be found in my private garden.	paɪnz kæn biː faʊnd ɪn maɪ ˈpraɪvɪt ˈɡɑːdn.
q	ai i	i	ˈkwaɪət	quiet	安靜	Liz is quiet in the school library.	lɪz ɪz ˈkwaɪət ɪn ðə skuːl ˈlaɪbrəri.
r	ai i	i	raind	rind	樹皮	Is rind eaten by a lizard?	ɪz raɪnd ˈiːtn baɪ ə ˈlɪzəd?

子音	母音	字母	IPA	生字	解釋	創作句子	IPA
s	ai i	i	said	side	側邊	That side of house is covered with ice.	ðæt saɪd ɒv haʊs ɪz ˈkʌvəd wɪð aɪs.
t	əʊ o	o	təʊ	toe	腳趾	Baby's toe is hurt when playing on a slide.	ˈbeɪbiz təʊ ɪz hɜːt wɛn ˈpleɪɪŋ ɒn ə slaɪd.
v	əʊ o	o	vəʊg	vogue	時尚	That model is vogue in her style.	ðæt ˈmɒdl ɪz vəʊg ɪn hɜː staɪl.
w	əʊ o	o	wəʊnt	wont	習慣於	She is wont in working hard.	ʃiː ɪz wəʊnt ɪn ˈwɜːkɪŋ hɑːd.
x	/	/	/	/	/	/	/
y	juː u	ou	juːθ	youth	青年	Youth is the symbol of an energetic spirit.	juːθ ɪz ðə ˈsɪmbəl ɒv ən ˌɛnəˈdʒɛtɪk ˈspɪrɪt.
z	iː e	e	ˈziːbrə	zebra	斑馬	Students walk across the zebra crossing with ease.	ˈstjuːdənts wɔːk əˈkrɒs ðə ˈziːbrə ˈkrɒsɪŋ wɪð iːz.

B. 持之以恆的練習方法

❶ 習慣聆聽及朗讀 IPA 圖表 ——主要讀準母音及子音，因為英語是一個重音計拍的語言。

❷ 讀字時要有節奏，留意重音的位置，同時聆聽他人說話時的語速，觀察嘴唇的移動情況。

❸ 一些語言如廣東話是沒有 r 和 th 音，所以非英語為母語的人是較難掌握標準的英語發音。

❹ 要特別注意英語生字的音節（syllable）及重音（stress）。由於重音會出現在生字不同的位置上，所以英語讀得有否成效，關鍵在於要熟悉自己的聲線，每天錄下聲音朗讀的功課作比較及加以改進，這樣學習效果必能快見成效。

❺ 朋輩亦可組成英語演說家學習群組，時刻加強鍛煉發音、單字及文法等技巧，配以電影欣賞和參與口語及詩詞朗誦比賽，成為傑出的演說者指日可待。

CHAPTER

3

場景練習篇

透過日常生活中不同的場景，
父母可引領子女探索及發掘不同的感受，
以輕鬆的心態互相磨合、溝通，
關係融洽，英語溝通自然能順暢地進行。
子女於場景中也能學習西方的文化、禮儀等，
加深英語的語境，說起英語來更自然及投入。

LESSON 6

SUBJECT: _____   DATE: _____

OBJECTIVES:

一起烹飪樂

　　烹飪，是一件很愉快的事。從選購食材開始，父母跟子女一起學習英語食材字詞之餘，也能跟隨每個烹調步驟，投入輕鬆的環境來說英語，從整個烹調過程中找到更多有趣的話題，加深學習英語的樂趣，並訓練小朋友以英語思考的能力。

NOTES

❶ **建立彼此的關係** ——無論是親子或朋輩，透過烹調可建立良好的溝通關係，贏得友誼及親情，發揮創意靈感，打開話匣子。

❷ **獲得讚賞** ——在煮食的過程中，能獲得父母或朋輩的稱讚，是對孩子的一份肯定，加強信心及成功感，正面的能量是加強說英語的強心針。

③ **擴闊社交圈子** ——與家人或朋友一起烹調，有説有笑，充實心靈，一起談天説地，認識更多身邊人，也能改善小孩被動、害羞的性格。

④ **認識英語生字及外國文化** ——加深認識材料、做法的生字，對外國飲食文化也增進不少了解，例如認識傳統的聖誕美食（roast turkey, roast ham）、英國的聖誕甜點（Christmas cake, Christmas pudding, mince pies），以及最受歡迎的聖誕食品（fruit cake, pumpkin pie, special Christmas cookies）。

⑤ **感受生活的小趣味** ——在烹調的過程中，總會發生不少趣事或小插曲，這些將成為説英語的話題，令説話溝通更和洽、更富趣味性。

TIPS

① 多抽空陪伴 ——假日空餘時，多抽空一起逛超級市場或菜市場，認識不同的食材，或一起搜集食譜及下廚，製造更多共同話題，為日後的英語溝通製造題材。

② 給予鼓勵 ——完成一道美食後，父母鼓勵的說話是對子女最大的肯定，令他們更有動力完成下一次目標。任何人都喜歡被人稱讚。

③ 分享及總結 ——用英語分享烹飪中的小趣味，既可分享生活之點滴，又可加強英語的聽、說能力。父母可以身作則，為孩子樹立好榜樣。

TRAINING

Little English Speakers: Lilian (L) and Pink (P)

P: It's Christmas time, so as my birthday! It's my favourite time of the year! I cherish this year most in my life.

L: Congratulations, and I'm glad to hear that. How will you celebrate, and whom will you celebrate with? Which of your our college boy friends will be here? Patrick or Michael?

P: Don't tease me! I feel so embarrassed. Lilian, to be honest, I couldn't even speak when I met new friends at home gatherings before. I preferred hiding in the kitchen.

L: Pink, I can hardly believe it. You are outgoing and always share your cooking techniques with others. You are truly amazing! What's the secret? Magic?

P: The "magic" is our Miss Chan. Christmas Eve is also Miss Chan's birthday. Once, she invited me to her birthday celebration at her home. She introduced me to her friends, relatives and neighbours and then took me to her kitchen where her cookbooks, utensils, and special herbs and ingredients were laid out, ready for cooking. Once she started cooking, children and friends came in one by one to chat with her about what she was doing. Her charisma and warmth inspire me a lot, so I started to treat her as my role model. I will always learn from her.

L: I am impressed by how much Miss Chan has influenced you. How did you tackle your speaking problem?

P: Well, it was hard at the beginning. But when I began to chit-chat about my recipes with others, such as the recipes for making Shepherd's Pie, Christmas cookies and puddings, my friends and I started talking and laughing together. With Miss Chan's encouragement, I decided to participate in the Recitation Day later on.

L: Great! We will be participating together.

P: Let's try our best!

EXERCISE

A. 閱讀理解

1. Where are Pink and Lilian?

2. Describe how Pink has learned to speak confidently. How does she feel about speaking now? Why?

3. According to Pink, how did Miss Chan influence her?

4. How do you approach your difficulties when it comes to speaking? Is it as same as Pink's?

5. Name five dishes that you like and write a recipe for each.

B. 朗讀生字

Words	IPA	中文解釋
kitchen	/ˈkɪtʃ.ən/	廚房
dessert	/dɪˈzɜːt/	甜品
pudding	/ˈpʊd.ɪŋ/	布甸
turkey	/ˈtɜː.ki/	火雞
dish	/dɪʃ/	菜式
outspoken	/ˌaʊtˈspəʊ.kən/	外向
cookbook	/ˈkʊk.bʊk/	烹飪書
utensils	/juːˈten.sɪl/	廚具
inspire	/ɪnˈspaɪər/	感動

C. 日常練習

1. Read the above dialogue aloud and record it.

2. Use the words above to create a story for personal presentation.

美心老師格言

成功有很多方法，但只有
勇於嘗試、實踐及定時檢
討，才是成功的好方法。

教孩子說 一口流利英語

場景練習篇

LESSON 7

SUBJECT:

DATE:

OBJECTIVES:

走進西式餐廳，輕鬆學英語

　　學習英語不一定在教室，通過不同的場景可加強聽、説英語的能力，並在特定的場景加深認識外國人的溝通、語調及待客之道，是很好的英語實地訓練課。

NOTES
學習要點

❶ **了解語境文化** ——除了認識餐牌字詞之外，置身於餐廳內，小朋友容易被場景氣圍感染，從而能夠融入場景文化當中，感受外地用餐的樂趣。

❷ **學習外國人口語用詞** ——外國人談話沒有冗長的語句，字詞簡潔、明快，參考外籍人士的説話語調，可加強説英語的地道性。

❸ **體會外國禮儀** ——即使不出國，到地道的西餐廳進餐，亦為小朋友提供一個學習外國人用餐禮儀及態度的機會，讓他們恍如置身外地餐廳，完全投入英語的說話語境。

TIPS

❶ **鼓勵子女多聽、多說** ——引導子女細心聆聽外籍人士的用語及語調，鼓勵他們勇敢地多說、多練習，自然學會更多說英語技巧及詞彙。

❷ **角色扮演** ——在家可以來個角色扮演的遊戲，化身侍應及食客，全程以英語溝通對話，令子女加深印象，寓玩於學。

TRAINING

Venue: A Western restaurant

Characters: Miss Chan (MC), Susie (S) - a young British woman

They have come to a seaside restaurant for dinner.

Waiter: Here's a seaside table for you. And here's your menu. Please also take a look at the set menu specials.

S: This is great. The sea breeze makes it very comfortable. Miss Chan, what would you like to order?

MC: The set meal with a French salad.

S: It sounds good to me. It's my favourite.

S: (Calling the waiter) Excuse me, may I please see the takeaway menu? I'd like to place an order for a fish burger, iced tea and chips for two.

NOTES

. . . .

EXERCISE

A. 閱讀理解

1. Who is dining with Miss Chan?

2. Where the restaurant is situated?

3. What dish had Miss Chan ordered?

4. What is the takeaway order from Susie?

5. Have you ever had dinner in a Western restaurant? Describe your experience.

B. 朗讀生字

Words	IPA	中文解釋
Shepherd's pie	/ˌʃep.ədzˈ paɪ/	肉餡 馬鈴薯泥餅
seafood	/ˈsiː.fuːd/	海鮮
tomato sauce	/təˈmɑː.təʊ/ /sɔːs/	番茄醬
cuisine	/kwɪˈziːn/	菜式
meal	/mɪəl/	飯餐
main course	/ˌmeɪn/ /ˈkɔːs/	主菜
mashed potatoes	/ˌmæʃt pəˈteɪ/ /təʊz/	薯茸
meat	/miːt/	肉類
fish and chips	/ˌfɪʃ/ /en/ /ˈtʃɪps/	炸魚薯條

roast beef and Yorkshire Pudding	/rəʊst/ /ˈbiː.f/ /ænd/ /ˈjɔːk.ʃər/ /ˈpʊd.ɪŋ/	烤牛肉與約克郡布丁
Trifle	/ˈtraɪ.fəl/	水果鬆糕
Banger and Mash	/ˈbæŋə(r)/ /ænd/ /mæʃ/	香腸佐薯茸
onion	/ˈʌn.jən/	洋葱
olive oil	/ˈɒl.ɪv/ /ˈɔɪl/	橄欖油
plain flour	/ˌpleɪn/ /ˈflaʊər/	麵粉
traditional	/trəˈdɪʃ.ən.əl/	傳統
chicken stock	/ˈtʃɪk.ɪn/ /stɒk/	雞湯
butter	/ˈbʌt.ər/	牛油

C. 日常練習

1. Read the dialogue aloud once and record it.

2. Use the words above for a story presentation.

香港是一個美食天堂，請説出以下菜式食物的味道：Chinese cuisine, Korean cuisine, Japanese cuisine, Vietnamese cuisine, Singapore cuisine, British cuisine

建議詞語

awful	/ˈɔː.fəl/	恐怖
overcooked	/ˌəʊ.vəˈkʊk/	過熟
amazing	/əˈmeɪ.zɪŋ/	驚訝
texture	/ˈteks.tʃər/	質感
crumbly	/ˈkrʌm.bəl.i/	鬆脆
roast	/rəʊst/	燒烤
tender	/ˈten.dər/	軟嫩
mushy	/ˈmʌʃ.i/	糊狀
soft	/sɒft/	軟滑
chewy	/ˈtʃuː.i/	耐嚼

LESSON 8

SUBJECT: _____ DATE: _____

OBJECTIVES:

參與公益活動，寓學習於助人

　　透過外出進行慈善活動，例如賣旗、派飯、表演等，除了練習英語會話之外，也可藉此學習溝通及組織活動的能力。家長甚至亦可一同參與，帶動子女多說英語。

NOTES
學習要點

1. **實地演說的機會** ——進行個人準備及技巧訓練前，不妨來一次面對群眾的演練，學生以英語為媒介，從策劃、提出意見到活動後改善之處，可訓練英語溝通，是一次很好的演練及互動。

2. **以生命帶動生命** ——抱着一顆善良的心，家長與子女一起走入社群，幫助身邊需要協助的人，以大手牽小手，一起來感受生命的意義。

TIPS

家長錦囊

① **家長以身作則** ——家長主動帶領子女面向社會群眾,如賣旗時與外籍人士溝通,透過簡單的説話交流,給予子女學習的榜樣。

② **傾聽子女的意見** ——策劃活動或進行活動演練時,家長留心小朋友提出的意見,並予以鼓勵,給予空間他們去實踐。

③ **良好的親子關係是學好英語的契機** ——小朋友喜歡父母一起參與,共同完成目標,在公益活動的過程中,愉快的親子氣氛令小朋友願意多説、多學習,邁出重要的一步。

TRAINING

Miss Chan (MC), Kami (K), Avis(A), Charlie(C), Heather (H) and Fan (F), a parent who is helping out.

MC: Hi, everybody, I have to give special thanks to all of you: Kami, Avis, Charlie, Heather and Fan. Having finished distributing the free rice boxes to the elderly, the poory and needy during the summer vacation, do you have any suggestions or improvements to share this time?

F: Miss Chan, although the weather is hot and the rice boxes are heavy, Charlie, Avis and Kami did it all so well. The elderly also appreciated the plays we put on for them.

C: Thanks, Fan. Due to our tight school schedule, we could not attend all the preparation meetings. We know that communication skills with classmates and volunteers are important for putting on plays and flag selling. Other learning experience opportunities can be learnt quickly outside school. By the way, we owe a debt of gratitude to the parent helpers for their kindness and support.

MC: That's great. Heather, I know that you have class training experience. Would you please share it with us?

H: Yes, Miss Chan. After graduating from my primary school, you selected me to be your Training Assistant. It's exciting and challenging because I have to deal with different tasks, such as administrative and training plans. Making schedules and activity leaflets as well as creating promotional materials and meeting with parents, time management was a real challenge in the beginning. Still, I have improved a lot with the help of other volunteers and Miss Chan.

MC: Glad to hear that. Avis, let's say a few words.

A: I am hungry, so let's cheer.

All: Wow! Hurrah!!!

EXERCISE

A. 閱讀理解

1. Name five Little English Speakers who are attending the meeting.

2. What have they done in this project?

3. Why couldn't Charlie join the preparation meeting?

4. What volunteer work has Heather done for Miss Chan?

5. Have you done volunteer work before? Why? What did you participate in?

B. 朗讀生字

Words	IPA	中文解釋
charity project	/ˈtʃær.ə.ti/ /ˈprɒdʒ.ekt/	慈善項目
rice box	/raɪs/ /bɒks/	飯盒
tight	/taɪt/	緊逼
drama	/ˈdrɑː.mə/	戲劇
Flag selling	/flæg/ /ˈselɪŋ/	賣旗
other learning experience	/ˈʌð.ər/ /ˈlɜː.nɪŋ/ /ɪkˈspɪə.ri.əns/	課外學習經驗
leaflet	/ˈliː.flət/	宣傳單張
improve	/ɪmˈpruːv/	改進
handle	/ˈhæn.dəl/	處理

C. 日常練習

1. Read the dialogue aloud once and record it.

2. Use the words above to create a story for individual presentation.

NOTES

. . . .

CHAPTER

4

演說練習及比賽篇

整理了個人情緒、建立自信心，

也掌握說英語的技巧後，

要在台上流暢地用英語演說，

平日必須多進行演說練習，

注意台上的聲調、態度及演說規則，

自然能說出流利的英語演說。

LESSON 9

SUBJECT:

DATE:

OBJECTIVES: ☆

個人演練

NOTES

學習要點

在學習心態上：

❶ **想說就說，不用害怕錯誤** ——不要因為怕説錯話而不敢開口，按照自己喜好的題目來演説，對有興趣的題材，自然能順暢地説出來。

❷ **學習與同伴溝通，互相扶持** ——站在課堂的講台上，縱然有些同伴會説出一些負面的説話，但緊記調節自己的心態，集中精神清楚地演説，與同伴互相交流，互補不足。

在演説準備上：

❶ **定下講題，撰寫講稿** ——以自己有興趣的題材為主，設定題目，預先撰寫稿子，修飾詞彙，令講稿簡潔、明快，言之有物。

②控制聲音語調 ——練習時控制自己的聲調、説話速度，不愠不趕，語氣平和、聲線鏗鏘。建議練習時為自己計算演説時間，不斷練習及比較，以改善語調速度。

③鍛煉用氣及發音 ——錄下自己的英文發音、高低音，不斷重複練習，找出自己能控制的音調。

④找合適的地方練習 ——練習初期可選擇浴室、睡房；中段期間可於公園、課室或客廳，以鍛煉聲音、語氣；後期可在禮堂、表演台，循序漸進，給予自己演説的信心。

熟習台上演説規則：

① 平衡自己的情緒。

② 姿勢要挺直。

③ 視線望向遠處。

④ 鞠躬及面向觀眾微笑。

⑤ 自然、有自信地朗誦詩篇或説英語。

⑥ 鞠躬及感謝觀眾的支持。

TRAINING

對 話 練 習

Miss Chan (MC)

Little English Speaker: Heather (H)

MC: Heather, which topic are you going to share with us?

H: My face. (Laughs) Whenever I see my face in the mirror, it looks quite oily sometimes. I use a cleanser to wash my face twice, then I brush my teeth and shower afterwards.

MC: It's good to describe your daily hygiene routine. How do you feel about your eyes, nose, and mouth?

H: My eyes are big and sparkling. Whenever I watch comedy or horror film, they'll fill with tears. I cry when my mother blames me for being lazy when it comes to my homework. My tears will fall down drop by drop. (Everybody laughs.)

MC: Heather, you know facial expression is important to all trainees before standing on the stage. Good eye contact and a lovely speaker's voice like yours will make a very positive impression on the adjudicators.

H: Are there forms of speaking that I need to learn?

MC: Reading poetry can train your understanding an author's thoughts and convey their ideas and emotions to the audience. But it's a big step and for the time being, concentrate on training on your biggest asset, your face.

H: Thank you, Miss Chan.

EXERCISE

A. 閱讀理解

1. Who is the Little English Speaker in this lesson? What topic does she want to share?

2. How does Heather describe her daily routine to keep her oily skin clean?

3. According to Miss Chan, why is facial expression so important to learn?

4. Name one form of public speaking.

5. Please describe your face and how you care for it.

B. 朗讀生字

Words	IPA	中文解釋
face	/feɪs/	面部 / 面孔
facial expression	/ˈfeɪ.ʃəl/ /ɪkˈspreʃ.ən/	面部表情
mirror	/ˈmɪr.ər/	鏡子
strange	/streɪndʒ/	古怪
stage	/steɪdʒ/	舞台
eye contact	/aɪ/ /ˈkɒn.tækt/	眼神接觸
sweet voice	/swiːt/ /vɔɪs/	甜美聲線
poem speaking	/ˈpəʊ.ɪm/ /ˈspiː.kɪŋ/	朗讀詩詞
author	/ˈɔː.θər/	作者

C. 日常練習

1. Read the dialogue aloud once and record it.

2. Use the words above to create a story for your individual presentation.

美心老師格言

每天愛自己、讚賞自己的聲線。

NOTES

LESSON 10

SUBJECT:

DATE:

OBJECTIVES: ☆

集體演練

NOTES

❶ 組員互相切磋 ——以 4 人、6 人、8 人或 10 人為一組，一起進行唸詩、對話等英語練習，互相交流技巧及意見。

❷ 掌握時間控制 ——演說的時間有限，妥善掌控自己演說的時間，不宜長篇大論，否則影響同組同伴的表現。

❸ 按照老師的意見改善 ——導師從旁留意各組員的表現，建議小朋友虛心聆聽導師有關說話技巧、語調、聲線、速度等，適度地作出調整，為未來的演說打好基礎。

熟習台上演說規則：

① 平衡自己的情緒。

② 姿勢要挺直。

③ 視線望向遠處。

④ 鞠躬及面向觀眾微笑。

⑤ 自然、有自信地朗誦詩篇或說英語。

⑥ 鞠躬及感謝觀眾的支持。

TRAINING

Voice drills, rehearsals how to follow the Trainers' instructions

Dialogue Training (1) Drills

Miss Chan (MC)

Joey (J) - a Training Assistant

Little English Speakers: Ken (K) and Mark (M)

K: Mark, although Miss Chan is always kind, I am still nervous when standing in front of her.

M: Come on! Take it easy! It is not a prison. It is a stage where you can see your improvement and keep on shining in your life. Never miss it.

MC: Wow! Today we're having a class drill. Everyone can have a chance to express themselves. Joey, any rundown for the afternoon's schedule?

J: Miss Chan, here you are. (Pointing to the schedule.) The red label is for Little English Speakers Assessment. Each trainee will have five minutes to present.

J: Hi all, I'm Joey Tang. Thank you for joining our Little English Speakers Drill Day-Elementary. Those who have passed the Drill Test will be allowed to participate in the summer competition. English Speaker Awards will be presented to those who achieve an "Honour" grade in the round.

(The drill test is in progress and finishes.)

J: Miss Chan, any suggestions for the speakers on the floor?

MC: Well, frankly speaking, it's pretty good for the first attempt. Still, when you drill at home or elsewhere again, make sure that you can control your vocal volume and pace when performing your speech. Never rush or shout, feel the flow yourself and try to feel at ease during your performance. And most importantly, always enjoy your moment on stage. I look forward to seeing all your remarkable achievements.

(All clap loudly and leave with confidence.)

EXERCISE

理解及練習

A. 閱讀理解

1. Who is nervous when facing Miss Chan?

2. Who comforts Ken, and what does he say?

3. Is it easy to get an English Speaker Award? What do you think?

4. What is Miss Chan's comment on the students' drill performance?

5. Assume you are Joey Tang and are assigned to organise a speaking competition. Write down the event rundown.

B. 朗讀生字

Words	IPA	中文解釋
afraid	/əˈfreɪd/	害怕
relaxed	/rɪˈlækst/	放鬆
express	/ɪkˈspres/	表達
rundown	/ˈrʌn.daʊn/	流程
first attempt	/ˈfɜːst/ /əˈtempt/	第一次
clap	/klæp/	拍掌
thunder	/ˈθʌn.dər/	如雷
natural	/ˈnætʃ.ər.əl/	自然
remarkable	/rɪˈmɑː.kə.bəl/	傑出

C. 日常練習

1. Read the dialogue aloud once and record it.

2. Use the words above to create a story for your individual presentation.

NOTES

. . . .

TRAINING

對話練習

Miss Chan (MC)

Little English Speakers: Mike (M), Andrew (A), Stephen (S) and Charlotte (C)

MC: Hi all! Throughout these training courses, what have you learnt about English speaking?

M: (Holds up his fingers to count.) Being Miss Chan's Little English Speakers, we must be polite, friendly and always smile at others. One thing is important: speak simple English like me. (All burst into laughter.)

A: Wow, it's been sunny all day. Time flies and it is Day 11 of Root Up Weeds and Watering. Look at me, do I look like a farmer? Ha ha ha!

C: Miss Chan has taught us how to speak confidently in three situations. Stephen, do you remember them?

S: Of course. I was shy in both private and public settings in the beginning, so I started to sing songs like "Do a deer, a female deer....." in the shower so I could memorise the rhythm and pace of the melody without fear. Then using my habit drills, when I am on the stage, all the words seem to come out from my brain without hesitation.

A: So do I. Before, when I talked with foreigners, I would start trembling and shaking. But when Miss Chan told me that my interests can also help with English speaking, I tried making a dish called Shepherd's Pie. As I cooked, I talked a lot about the ingredients and the necessary cooking skill. I shared them with my friend who was helping me. My oral skills are better and I speak more fluently.

Miss Chan: I love to hear that. Let's go watering first.

EXERCISE

理解及練習

A. 閱讀理解

1. What is LES? Who are they and what are their personal qualities?

2. As a LES, what was Stephen's learning experience like after consultating with Miss Chan?

3. How did Andrew solve his speaking problem? Is it similar to yours? Please describe your experiences.

4. Have you ever joined any volunteer activities such as visiting an organic farm before? Name them and describe the roles you were responsible for.

5. Have you tried speaking techniques like Stephen's and Andrew's? Describe yours.

B. 朗讀生字

Words	IPA	中文解釋
polite	/pəˈlaɪt/	禮貌
friendly	/ˈfrend.li/	友善
smile	/smaɪl/	微笑
private	/ˈpraɪ.vət/	私人
public	/ˈpʌb.lɪk/	公眾
ingredients	/ɪnˈɡriː.di.ənt/	材料
brain	/breɪn/	頭腦
hesitation	/ˌhez.ɪˈteɪ.ʃən/	猶疑
responsible	/rɪˈspɒn.sə.bəl/	負責

C. 日常練習

1. Read the dialogue aloud once and record it.

2. Use the words above to create a story for your individual presentation.

美心老師格言

不斷學習和改善，就是尋找心中的自己。

LESSON 11

OBJECTIVES:

英語演說比賽日

NOTES

比賽前一天準備:

❶ **充足的作息時間** ——養成早睡早起的習慣,讓心肺及身體得到充足的休息,以免過勞的生活習慣影響喉嚨及聲線。

❷ **多喝暖水** ——平時以暖水為主,讓喉嚨保持濕潤,也能保持心肺功能健康。

❸ **以柔軟運動為主** ——為了減輕比賽前的壓力,適宜讓小朋友做些柔軟的運動,以紓緩身體的肌肉,別以劇烈運動為主,以免肌肉過於勞累而影響表現。

❹ **毋須死背誦材** ——內容已牢牢記在腦內，這時毋須再死背硬記，最重要是明白內容的要點，感受氣氛，將文章內的精髓盡情地表達出來，吸引觀眾的注意，引起共鳴。

比賽當天：

❶ **在台上踏台板** ——如許可的話，嘗試在舞台上演練一次，熟習舞台上的位置、氣氛等等，細聽清楚自己的聲音、呼吸節奏，為比賽做好最後準備。

❷ **保持聲音鏗鏘** ——聲音要集中、有力、清晰及突出，配合身體語言的表達，充分展現誦材內容的喜怒哀樂。

❸ **表達內容的核心意義** ——了解文章的深層意義，運用眼神、身體語言、聲調、節奏、藝術性等演繹作者的想法及意思，賦予文章靈魂。

❹ **適當的停頓** —— 在演說時作出恰當的停頓位置，給人一種從容的感覺，不讓別人感到自己緊張的情緒。

❺ **放鬆、再放鬆** ——在比賽前，有參賽者會與評判交流一下，以幫助自己的聲音熟習，甚至得到放鬆的機會；又或是可靜靜地在一旁，讓自己安靜心神，理清思緒。

❻ **合適的衣着** ——不要穿得過於臃腫，或會阻礙肢體的表現。簡單的恤衫或裙子，已能夠表達你的尊重。

　　陳老師提提你，英語演説時最重要留意以下幾個部分：

- **肢體語言** ——眼神、肢體動作、鎮靜。
- **聲音** ——音量、説話節奏、發音、語調。
- **藝術表演性** ——演繹內容的觀賞性。

如何挑選比賽優勝者？

在表演台上，聲線的運用及表演者的自信是十分重要的。如同學們在練習誦材時能謹記以下重點，成績一定突飛猛進。

❶ 是否運用詩的語言吸引觀眾？

❷ 有帶領觀眾更好地了解誦材嗎？

❸ 有了解自己聲音的特點，為詩詞注入生命力嗎？

❹ 你的表演能為詩詞作出敬意嗎？

如能做到讓觀眾通過你的演譯，能與作者的心意連結在一起，就是傑出的表演者。

TRAINING

對話練習

Miss Chan (MC)

Charlie (C), Shirley (S)

MC: Today is the big day of the speaking competition. Thank you for being the adjudicator assistant.

C: It's my great pleasure. Miss Chan, please be seated. Good morning (He faces the audience), the honourable Adjudicator Miss Chan, parents and classmates. Before we start our Speaking Day, please set your phone or any other devices to silent mode. Please do not leave or enter the training room during the competition. The first speaker is Melissa. Please come to the stage. Your sharing topic is "Popcorn".

....

After the competition:

S: Miss Chan, the children performed really well today, like this one who performed the poem "Popcorn". She really looks like popcorn, doesn't she?

MC: Shirley, that is a good observation. Adjudicators will use the marking reference and rate the overall comments as unsatisfactory, pass, proficiency, merit or honour to participants afterwards.

Physical Presence	Voice	Artistry
Eye contact/ body language	Volume/ pace and rhythm	Interpretation
Poise/ command	Articulation/ intonation	

S: Never shout when performing. Don't wriggle or lean forward. Don't say words too slowly and over-stress words when speaking on stage. I'll remember your words.

MC: Good.

C: The whole event proved an enjoyable and absorbing end to our work. Let's take photos. Say "cheese" !

A. 閱讀理解

1. Who was the Master of Ceremonies on English Speaking Day ?

2. Name two rules that the audience must follow during the competition.

3. Name three criteria used in the marking scheme.

4. What does "wriggle" mean? Why would you wriggle in the competition?

5. Imagine that you are the emcee. Write a speaking script in 100 words.

B. 朗讀生字

Words	IPA	中文解釋
rising tone	/ˈraɪ.zɪŋ/ /təʊn/	升調
falling tone	/ˈfɔː.lɪŋ/ /təʊn/	降調
character	/ˈkær.ək.tər/	角色
rush	/rʌʃ/	匆忙
shout	/ʃaʊt/	大叫
from your heart	/frəm/ /jɔːr/ /hɑːt/	發自內心
volume	/ˈvɒl.juːm/	聲量
speed	/spiːd/	速度
facial expression	/ˈfeɪ.ʃəl/ /ɪkˈspreʃ.ən/	面部表情

C. 日常練習

1. Read the dialogue aloud once and record it.

2. Use the words above to create a story for your individual presentation.

NOTES

. . . .

LESSON 12

SUBJECT: DATE:

OBJECTIVES:

如何保持學講英語的信心？

要讓小朋友保持一份說英語的自信心，父母及師長必須加以引導及給予鼓勵，父母的參與實在必不可少。

NOTES

❶ **保持心境開朗及放鬆** ——懷着一份開心愉快的心情，說起英語來都會稱心如意。如運用適當的英語來表達自己，內心也會感到無比愉快，對學習有正面的幫助。

❷ **我口講我心** ——說英語時按自己內心的感受及所想，會減少不必要的不安感。

❸ **學習自我控制及時間管理** ——學習英文技巧需要長時間練習，持之以恆，控制自己的情緒，別被情緒打垮。

④ **訂立目標**——確定了説英語的決心及目標後，逐步向着這個目標前進，説英語的技巧會提高不少。

TIPS

① **與子女說故事**——小朋友喜歡色彩繽紛、故事吸引的繪本，父母引導式的問題能訓練小朋友的聲調、語調及運用英語字詞的技巧，為他們奠下基礎。

② **每天 15 分鐘說英語時間**——每天安排特定説英語時間，給子女學習英語的習慣，循序漸進説起英語。

③ **生活遊戲學英語**——日常與子女玩桌遊，或入廚煮食時，不妨以英語作為溝通媒介，由遊玩中學習，引起他們的興趣，小朋友會感到非常有趣味而用心學習。

④ **有聲書及傳播媒體**——透過有聲書或其他網上媒體，多聽多説，能夠提升説英語的熟練性及流暢性。

後記

　　此書着重訓練孩子自發性地輕鬆說英語，互動性地體驗生活英語的樂趣。

　　說英語，是與他人溝通的一項工具。我編寫此書之目的，是希望藉本書的幫助，讓孩子掌握基本英語說話的要求及學習運用英語口語技巧的能力，特別適合想提升英語說話能力的朋友、青少年、家長與幼稚園及小學生一起研習。

　　希望大家隨着此書體驗過後，一起愉快地說英語、談理想。

　　藉此，我也特別感謝為本書付出努力的Heather Chiu、Charlie Yeung、Aiden、Jessica、Morris Cheung 及其他學員。

學生感謝語*

My name is Charlie Yeung, a grade-12 student who partnered with Heather in assisting our teacher and mentor—Miss Annie Chan Mei Sum—in both teaching and administration.

In Hong Kong, the importance of using the English language is uttered subtly, but at once, completely, in many different ways. Ranging from signposts to menus, the prevalence of English is rather obvious and omnipresent that we might actually be diminished if the language is taken away from us.

At the age of 18, many students in Hong Kong are competing against each other for a place at the universities in Hong Kong. Among the subjects tested in the entrance exam, English language is the one that failed many pupils in allowing them a place to study there.

In the short term, it's vital for us to pass in the English language in order to get ourselves into any one of the universities here in Hong Kong.

In the long term, this language possesses the ability to get us to different corners of the world and broaden our horizons on multiple levels. Throughout our lives, English can actually be our asset in taking us to places we never thought we could've been.

Though it may all sound very cliché, it's still the truth.

Compared to Heather, the daughter of Miss Chan, I should humbly say that I know very little about our teacher. Nevertheless, her glorious virtues of educating everyone, no matter young and old, rich or poor, are esteemed.

I could still recall the time when I got an answer from her that stirred up admiration in me after asking her this question. "Why could you give up on being a lawyer and choose to become an English trainer?"

She gently answered that her heart has always been and will always be for nurturing and teaching people in improving their English proficiency.

That's the moment that I knew she is the figure and role model people could look up to and hold onto.

Charlie Yeung
(English Speaker in Annie Training Centre)

Hello, I am Avis Yan. I am a Primary 5 student. I think English is important as Chinese in Hong Kong. Hong Kong is an international city and commercial centre. You always need to communicate with people from different countries. In addition to Chinese, English is essential in our daily life.

Miss Chan is my mentoring teacher. When I was in kindergarten, my mum helped me to enroll her English lessons. Miss Chan guided me very well. There is lots of fun during the lessons. Dramas, wording competitions and other extraordinary activities made learning English interesting. From that on, I found that I love English. She made my day.

Miss Chan is kind and keen to help children. Miss Chan helps students that are in need in English. She hopes every student can learn English easily. She is willing to provide non-profit making service to those cannot afford for tutors. Then, children who have financial difficulties just need to pay very little. I am very appreciate her.

In short, my English improved a lot because Miss Chan directed me very well. A good language needs to accumulate over a long period of time, it cannot advance by leaps and bounds.

Avis Yan
(Little English Speaker in Annie Training Centre)

117

Hi, everyone. My name is Winson Yan, a college student right now. I am honored to write this quoted passage for my teacher Miss Chan.

I met Miss Chan through an English writing summer tutorial class in Tuen Mun Yan Oi Tong building when I was 11 years old. Also, Miss Chan's daughter is my primary schoolmate and my mum knew Miss Chan logically. Learning English is always challenging for me, then my mother found Miss Chan to be my English teacher and Miss Chan accompanied me through my junior high school period. As a result, I had learnt a lot of useful English language skills from Miss Chan.

In my personal situation, English language skills are an indispensable skill for me since all the college courses are teaching in English. If I do not have an English background it would be extremely hard for me and I will have a high chance of failing the test. Furthermore, English language skills are necessary working skills in Hong Kong. It is related to your personal competitiveness. When I am doing my summer job I always need to communicate with the foreign customers and explain the details of products to them. My oral skill lets the customer and boss appreciate me, it can build my confidence!

As you can guess, I mainly learnt pronunciation and face to face oral skills from Miss Chan. She also helped me upgrade my English vocabulary and sentence structure to allow me to express myself precisely, like more complicated sentence structure and professional words.

All in all, practicing your English is worth it to anyone, it can help you find more opportunities and have a colorful life.

Winson Yan
(English Speaker in Annie Training Centre)

Hi everyone, I am Heather, a year one student majoring in Linguistics and Translation. Miss Chan is my mother, as well as my lifelong mentor.

Despite Chinese, English is nothing more familiar to me as Miss Chan's daughter. Since I was living in my mother's womb, she had taught me English not only by passing on knowledge to me, but also bringing me to all sorts of courses and conferences. Those experiences had inspired me to delve into language professionals.

Around primary 2-3, I started to volunteer as Miss Chan's teaching assistant. Everytime I would be amazed by how passionate and energetic Miss Chan was when it comes to teaching English. Instead of spoon-feeding children with English vocabularies or other information, she ought to teach them through playing games. Also, she would dig out one's interest and create teaching plan accordingly. As an experienced English teacher, who had devote herself in education career for more than 30 years, she knows what children need for English learning.

Throughout my 18-year-life, I had witnessed Miss Chan's effort paid in education. Every child deserves a mentor like her. I hope she could stay gold, and keep on affecting one's life with her own life.

Heather Chiu

* 為保留孩子們最真實的情感，以上文章以原文刊登。

參考書目

1. Clemen, G. D. B. (2003). *British and American Festivities*. The Commercial Press

2. Jones, D. (2011). *Cambridge English Pronouncing Dictionary (18th edition)*. Cambridge University Press

3. *Oxford Advanced Learner's Dictionary (9th edition)*. Oxford University Press

4, 湯恩比、池田大作 (2000)。《眺望人類新紀元》。天地圖書。

5. Wikihow

教孩子
說一口
流利英語
從建立自信、
認讀拼音到場景練習

著者
陳美心

責任編輯
簡詠怡

英文編輯
Joanna Hughes

裝幀設計
羅美齡

排版
辛紅梅、楊詠雯

出版者
萬里機構出版有限公司
香港北角英皇道 499 號北角工業大廈 20 樓
電話：2564 7511　　傳真：2565 5539
電郵：info@wanlibk.com
網址：http://www.wanlibk.com
　　　http://www.facebook.com/wanlibk

發行者
香港聯合書刊物流有限公司
香港荃灣德士古道 220-248 號荃灣工業中心 16 樓
電話：2150 2100　　傳真：2407 3062
電郵：info@suplogistics.com.hk
網址：http://www.suplogistics.com.hk

承印者
中華商務彩色印刷有限公司
香港新界大埔汀麗路 36 號

出版日期
二〇二二年一月第一次印刷

規格
大 32 開（210 mm × 142 mm）